THE **7** CONTINENTS

AUSTRALIA

APRIL PULLEY SAYRE

Twenty-First Century Books
Brookfield, Connecticut

For my nephew, David Turner Willett
—A.P.S.

Published by Twenty-First Century Books
A Division of The Millbrook Press, Inc.
2 Old New Milford Road
Brookfield, Connecticut 06804

Text copyright © 1998 by April Pulley Sayre
Maps by Joe LeMonnier
All rights reserved.

Library of Congress Cataloging-in-Publication Data

Sayre, April Pulley.
  Australia / April Pulley Sayre.
     p.   cm. —(The seven continents)
  Includes bibliographical references (p.   ) and index.
  Summary: Describes the geography of the continent of Austalia
    and the plants and animals that live there.
        ISBN 0-7613-3007-0 (alk. paper)
  1. Australia—Juvenile literature. [1. Australia. 2. Natural history—Australia.]
     I. Title. II. Series: Sayre, April Pulley. Seven continents.
  DU96.S27   1998
  994—dc21   97-35280
                                                                         CIP
                                                                          AC

Printed in the United States of America
5 4 3 2 1

Photo Credits

Cover photograph courtesy of © The Stock Market/David Ball.

Photographs courtesy of Gamma Liaison: pp. 8 (© David Austen), 36 (© James Pozarik); Australian Tourist Commission: pp. 12, 54; Animals Animals: pp. 16 (© Breck P. Kent), 31 (© Hans and Judy Beste); Photo Researchers: pp. 17 (© Mark Newman), 34 (© Dr. Paul A. Zahl), 38 (© Tom McHugh), 40 (© Joyce Photographics), 41 (top © Tom McHugh), 42 (© Mitch Reardon), 46 (top © 1973 Tom McHugh), 48 (© Bill Bachman); Woodfin Camp: pp. 19 (© David Austen), 24 (© Penny Tweedie), 29 (© Mike Yamashita); Peter Arnold, Inc.: pp. 20 (© Jean-Paul Ferrero/AUSCAPE), 26 (© Jean-Marc La Roque/AUSCAPE); Tom Stack & Associates: pp. 41 (bottom © Dave Watts), 46 (inset © John Shaw); Minden Pictures: p. 45 (© Shin Yoshino).

CONTENTS

Introduction   CONTINENTS: WHERE WE STAND   5

One   KEYS TO THE CONTINENT   9

Two   THE LAND DOWN UNDER   13

Three   THE NATURE OF AUSTRALIA   27

Four   MARVELOUS MARSUPIALS AND MONOTREMES   39

Five   THE RABBIT THAT ALMOST ATE AUSTRALIA . . . AND OTHER ANIMAL ISSUES   49

Glossary   56
Political Map of Australia   59
Further Reading   60
Index   62

INTRODUCTION

CONTINENTS: WHERE WE STAND

The ground you stand on may seem solid and stable, but it's really moving all the time. How is that possible? Because all of the earth's continents, islands, oceans, and people ride on tectonic plates. These plates, which are huge slabs of the earth's crust, float on top of hot, melted rock below. One plate may carry a whole continent and a piece of an ocean. Another may carry only a few islands and some ocean. The plates shift, slide, and even bump together as the molten rock below them flows.

Plate edges are where the action is, geologically speaking. That's where volcanoes erupt and earthquakes shake the land. Tectonic plates collide, gradually crumpling continents into folds that become mountains. Dry land, or ocean floor, can be made at these plate edges. Melted rock, spurting out of volcanoes or oozing out of cracks between plates, cools and solidifies. Dry land, or ocean floor, can also be destroyed here, as the edge of one tectonic plate slips underneath another. The moving, grinding plates create tremendous pressure and heat, which melts the rock, turning it into semisolid material.

Continents, the world's largest landmasses, the rock rafts where we live, ride on this shifting puzzle of tectonic plates. These continents are made of material that floated to the surface when much of the earth was hot and liquid long ago. The floating material then cooled and became solid. Two hundred and fifty million years ago, there was only one continent, the supercontinent Pangaea, surrounded by one ocean, Panthalassa. But since then, the tectonic plates have moved, breaking apart the continents and rearranging them. Today there are seven continents: North America, South America, Europe, Asia, Africa, Australia, and Antarctica.

250 Million Years Ago

Two hundred and fifty million years ago there was only one continent and one ocean, as shown above. (Rough shapes the continents would eventually take are outlined in black.) The view below shows where the seven continents are today. These positions will continue to change slowly as tectonic plates shift.

Present Day

Each continent has its own unique character and conditions, shaped by its history and position on the earth. Europe, which is connected to Asia, has lots of coastline and moist, ocean air. Australia, meanwhile, is influenced by its neighbor, Antarctica, which sends cool currents northward to its shores. North America and South America were once separated, but are now connected by Panama. Over the years, animals, from ancient camels to armadillos, have traveled the bridge between these two continents.

A continent's landscapes, geology, weather, and natural communities affect almost every human action taken on that continent, from planting a seed to waging a war. Rivers become the borders of countries. Soil determines what we can grow. Weather and climate affect our cultures—what we feel, how we dress, even how we celebrate.

Understanding continents can give us a deeper knowledge of the earth—its plants, animals, and people. It can help us see behind news headlines to appreciate the forces that shape world events. Such knowledge can be helpful, especially in a world that's constantly changing and shifting, down to the very earth beneath our feet.

Golfers at a course in Queensland, Australia, are frequently interrupted by curious kangaroos.

ONE

KEYS TO THE CONTINENT

When people describe Australia, certain words come up again and again. *Hot. Dry. Flat. Sandy. Harsh.* The vast interior of the continent is all of these things and more. It's unpredictable. One year the land may be bone dry, when not a drop of rain falls. Yet the next year, heavy rains may bring floods, creating roads too muddy to pass. Not everyone would choose to live under these harsh natural conditions. So it's no wonder that towns and people here are relatively few and far between.

There is, however, another Australia. Clinging to parts of the coastline are modern cities that thrive in the midst of green hillsides, grassy plains, and wet forests. Most Australians live in these green zones—where the weather and climate are moderated by moisture from the ocean. But even there, their lives, their habits, and their culture are still linked to the Outback—the hot, dry lands at the continent's heart.

As for Australia's animals, they take the prize for strangeness. Unless you're from Australia, of course. Then, it may seem perfectly natural to have a 7-foot- (2-meter-) tall animal hopping in your backyard. These animals, kangaroos, were a shock to early European visitors. So were many other Australian animals: wallabies, wombats, koalas, and more. Perhaps that's understandable. How would you react if an 8-foot-long (2.4-meter-long) monitor lizard came to your picnic or if a 120-pound (54-kilogram) bird, an emu, ran across your path?

One Australian native, the platypus, is so odd that some European scientists first thought the animal was a joke. The platypus has fur and claws like a beaver. But it also has webbed feet and a bill like a duck. In 1798, scientists at the British Museum received a stuffed specimen from explorers; but they thought it was bits of different animals sewn together!

Because Australia has so many extraordinary animals and plants, it's awfully easy for outsiders to treat it as just a museum of oddity. Fact is, Australia is a continent with a fascinating geology and climate. It supports intricate natural communities. It contains some of the world's oldest rocks, most ancient plants, and longest-surviving cultures. Who's to say that Australia's animals and plants aren't the "normal" ones, and that those in the rest of the world are the oddities?

THE BASICS

The continent of Australia lies in the Southern Hemisphere, between the Pacific and Indian Oceans, and covers 2,975,000 square miles (7,705,300 square kilometers). That makes it about the size of the lower 48 (continental) United States.

Australia is divided into six states and two territories. The six states are Queensland, South Australia, Western Australia, New South Wales, Tasmania, and Victoria. The two territories are the Northern Territory and the Australian Capital Territory, which is where the capital city, Canberra, is located.

Sunny, warm, flat, and low-lying, Australia is the flattest continent. Its average height above sea level is less than 1,000 feet (305 meters), and it has only one major mountain range, called the Great Dividing Range. The continent is sunny and warm, in general, because it is close to the equator. Yet up on its mountains, the weather can get cool enough for snow to fall.

CONTINENTAL CHARACTERISTICS

- It's summer in Australia when it's winter in North America. All Australia's seasons occur at opposite times to those of North America and Europe.
- Most of Australia is covered by desert or semidesert. Australians call these dry areas the Outback. Other parts of the continent are covered by savanna, which is grassland with widely separated trees. Australians call these and other, more wooded areas the Bush.
- Australia is famous for its Great Barrier Reef, which parallels the northeast coast of the continent. The Great Barrier Reef is the largest coral reef in the world.
- Australia is isolated from other continents, having no natural land bridges in between. Partly because of this isolation, many unique animals and plants are found in Australia.
- Australia has relatively few people. The land is the size of the continental United States, yet, with 18 million people, it has only 7 percent of the United States' population.

- Most of Australia's people live near its coasts, where the weather is cooler and wetter. Much of the interior of the continent is very sunny, hot, dry, and sparsely populated.
- Once a part of Great Britain, Australia is now an independent country.

World Records Held by Australia

- Smallest continent
- Flattest continent
- Lowest average elevation, or height above sea level
- Longest coral reef: 1,250 miles (2,000 kilometers)
- Second-driest continent (Antarctica is drier)
- Only continent without a high mountain range
- Sixth-largest country in the world, with 5 percent of the earth's land surface

Statistics and Records Within Australia

- Length of coastline: 22,776 miles (36,735 kilometers)
- Largest lake: Lake Eyre—3,590 square miles (9,300 square kilometers)
- Longest river system: Murray-Darling
- Longest river: Darling—1,750 miles (2,823 kilometers)
- Highest point: Mt. Kosciusko—7,316 feet (2,230 meters)
- Lowest point: Lake Eyre—39 feet (12 meters) below sea level
- Hottest place: Cloncurry, in Queensland, where the temperature hit 127°F (53°C) in 1889

Children in swim suits, not snowsuits, greet Santa Claus at an Australian beach resort.

TWO

THE LAND DOWN UNDER

Australia is often called "the Land Down Under." That's because it is down under, or south, of the equator. (The equator is the imaginary line that runs around the earth's middle.) Australia's location creates some effects that can seem a little strange to those of us above the equator in the Northern Hemisphere, in places such as North America, Europe, and Asia. But this southern location, plus a distinctive geology and climate, have set the stage for the evolution of Australia's extraordinary animals, plants, and cultures.

TWO TOPSY-TURVY THINGS ABOUT AUSTRALIA

We usually think that when we travel north, we'll find cooler climates. (Climate is a region's long-term weather.) For instance, it's much cooler in New York City than in Miami. But the opposite is true in Australia. The cooler cities, such as Melbourne, are down south. The warmer cities, such as Darwin, are to the north.

Why the turnabout? Because Australia is in the Southern Hemisphere, and the warmth or chilliness of a region's climate is affected in part by its latitude. (Latitude is a measurement of distance and position north or south of the equator.) Places near the poles are generally colder, and places near the equator are warmer. So in the Northern Hemisphere you would have to travel south to get closer to the equator and warmer weather. But in the Southern Hemisphere, you would have to travel north to reach warm, equatorial countries!

BACKWARD SEASONS

If you live in Australia, you might go to the beach for Christmas. And snow skiing would be better in July than in December. Why? Because in most of Australia, the seasons are just the opposite of those in North America. In Australia, spring begins in September. Summer starts in December. Autumn is in March. And winter arrives in June. These flip-flopped seasons are another consequence of Australia's location in the Southern Hemisphere.

Seasons are created by the motion of the earth and the sun, which perform a remarkable, spinning dance with one another. The earth spins around its own axis, an imaginary line that runs from the North Pole to the South Pole. At the same time, the earth also travels around the sun. There's one more crucial part to this dance: the earth's axis

GEOGRAPHIC WISDOM: POLAR, TEMPERATE, OR TROPICAL?

When you're talking about geography, three words pop up a lot: *tropical*, *temperate*, and *polar*. (There are tropical countries, polar bears, temperate zones, tropical rain forests—all sorts of examples!) These words are used to describe a region's latitude, in general, instead of using an actual measurement of latitude. Tropical, temperate, and polar regions are bounded by imaginary lines—lines of latitude that have been given special names. Here's how they work:

- Something polar is near the North or South Pole. Usually it's within the Arctic Circle or the Antarctic Circle.
- Anything tropical has to do with the regions near the equator—specifically between the tropic of Cancer and the tropic of Capricorn.
- The temperate zones are the "in-between places." They are in between the polar regions and the tropical regions. Specifically, the temperate region in the Northern Hemisphere is between the tropic of Cancer and the Arctic Circle. In the Southern Hemisphere, it's between the tropic of Capricorn and the Antarctic Circle.

Part of Australia lies in a temperate zone, the way most of North America does. These areas experience seasons: spring, summer, fall, and winter. But the northern part of Australia, often called the Top End, is tropical. It's close to the equator, where the day length is about the same year-round.

The Top End, also called the Tropical Monsoon Zone, doesn't have four seasons. Its two seasons are "the Wet" and "the Dry." The Wet, from October to March, is marked by monsoons—times of torrential rains and flooding. The Dry, from May to September, is marked by drought.

is tilted, relative to the sun. So as it travels around the sun, the amount of sunlight some parts of the earth receive changes, day to day. (If the earth weren't tilted on its axis, each part of the earth would get the same amount of sunlight every day. No region of the earth would have seasons.) At certain times of year, the Northern Hemisphere is closer to the sun than it is at other times. So it receives more direct sunlight and has more hours of sunlight. At this time, we have summer in North America. However, at the same time, the Southern Hemisphere is tilted away from the sun. So Australia, which is in the Southern Hemisphere, gets fewer hours of sunlight and thus experiences winter.

DISAPPEARING RIVERS AND THE LAY OF THE LAND

Australia has three main geographic regions: the eastern highlands, the central eastern lowlands, and the western plateau. Running along the east coast, from Cape York to the island of Tasmania, are the eastern highlands. This region is made up of a broken line of low, rounded mountains called the Great Dividing Range. To the west are the central eastern lowlands. These are true lowlands, only 1,148 feet (350 meters) above sea level. Farther to the west, making up three-quarters of the continent, is the western plateau. This raised area of flat, dry land is mostly desert and is often called the Outback.

YOU CALL THIS A MOUNTAIN?

If you like to climb high mountains, don't go to Australia. Most of the land is flat, and the mountains are very low. Australia's highest peak, Mt. Kosciusko, located in New South Wales, is merely 7,310 feet (2,228 meters) high. That's small, compared to the height of the Rocky Mountains or the Alps. Mt. Everest, for instance, at a height of 29,141 feet (8,882 meters), is four times higher than Australia's highest mountain!

Australia's mountains may be relatively low, but they're splendidly scenic, containing forests, cliffs, canyons, and waterfalls. The highest mountains, in southeastern Australia and on the island of Tasmania, receive snow in winter and have ski resorts. Some of the best are in the Snowy Mountains south of Canberra. Tasmania's mountains are jagged and wild, with beautiful lakes and rivers. Australia also has several other small mountain ranges, such as the Macdonnell, Hammersley, and Musgrave ranges. These rise up from the western plateau.

ONE BIG HUNK OF ROCK

Smack dab in the middle of Australia is a truly tremendous rock called Uluru. Uluru is a monolith, meaning it is a boulder made entirely of one rock. Uluru towers 1,140 feet (348 meters) above the ground and stretches almost 2 miles (3 kilometers) long. Only part of the rock is visible; most of it is buried below the ground. Visitors from all over the world come to hike their way up the rock. The rock's color changes throughout the day as the sun moves in the sky. At sunset, the rock seems to glow pink or red. Uluru is

The Great Dividing Range, seen in the distance, is the backbone of Australia's eastern highlands region.

a sacred place for the Aborigines, the people who first settled Australia. (For many years, Uluru was called Ayers Rock. When control of this site was returned to the Aborigines, they restored the rock's ancient, sacred name.)

In addition to Uluru, Australia has hundreds of other interesting rock formations. The Devil's Marbles, stacks of huge rounded boulders, lie north of Alice Springs. The Twelve Apostles, tremendous rock formations, can be found off the Victorian coast. The Bungle Bungles, which are smooth domes and pinnacles near the Kimberley Mountains of Western Australia, were created when soft sedimentary rocks eroded over hundreds of millions of years. The Pinnacles, rock pillars that stick up out of the sand in Nambung National Park, are proof that a forest once grew there. Water seeping along channels made by tree roots in the sand dunes created the Pinnacles long ago.

Climbing Uluru is not an easy task. Many tourists turn back before reaching the top.

DON'T DIVE IN

The seventeenth-largest lake in the world, Lake Eyre, is found in Australia. But don't go there for a swim without checking first. The lake may fill with water only once in fifty years! The huge floods that fill it occur after heavy rains. Most of the time the lake bed is dry, covered with bright white sheets of salty crust. When Lake Eyre does fill, the landscape changes dramatically, becoming a haven, green with plants and teeming with birds and other wildlife. Australia has relatively few other lakes; most are small and are located in the eastern highlands. But many, such as Lake Barrine, Dove Lake, and Blue Lake, are beautiful scenic spots.

RARE RIVERS

Many continents, such as Europe, are crisscrossed by rivers that flow all year long. Australia is different. It has very few rivers, and those are often dry for part of the year. They fill up only after heavy rains. Why are rivers so rare in Australia? Because very little of Australia's rainfall runs off into rivers. Much of the rainfall evaporates almost immediately off the ground, because of the hot, dry air. Or it percolates down into sand, sandstone, and limestone, which has lots of natural holes and caves. As a result, rainwater rarely reaches a riverbed.

CITIES THAT WERE BUILT ON ROCK

Water and weather are not the only factors that affect where Australians live. The key to the history of many Australian towns lies in the ground beneath them. Towns such as Broken Hill, Kalgoorlie, Bendigo, and many others are built around mineral mines and transportation routes. Australia is rich in minerals, including silver, opals, bauxite, gold, copper, iron ore, lead, tin, and uranium. In 1993, 40 percent of the world's diamonds came from Australia. Queensland is a major source of the world's bauxite, which is used in making aluminum. Mount Isa and the mines nearby, also in Queensland, provide more silver and lead than any other part of the world.

In the 1850s, Australia experienced "gold rushes," waves of settlers bent on making their fortune mining gold. They moved into small mining towns, later abandoning those towns when the gold veins had been stripped of whatever gold could be mined by hand. Today, large-scale mining operations dominate the industry, excavating precious minerals such as gold, and also producing coal and natural gas. Australia is one of the world's leading coal exporters. It's one more way that Australians are connected to their continent. Underneath the continent's hot, dry exterior, there's treasure to be found.

Lake Eyre is usually covered with a white salty crust. It may fill with water only two or three times in a century!

Small Australian rivers fringe the continent and flow into the sea. But Australia has only one really large river system, the Murray-Darling, located in the southeast. The Darling River dries up during droughts, so the Murray River is the longest "permanent" river in Australia. Yet even this massive river has dried up during the severest of droughts. When the rivers dry up, they leave behind small ponds called billabongs, made famous in the Australian folk song "Waltzing Matilda."

An Old, Peaceful Place

Geologically speaking, Australia is an old, quiet, worn-down land. In Australia, you can step on rocks more than 3 billion years old, some of the oldest rocks on earth. In addition to being old, Australia is geologically quiet. It doesn't have the strong earthquakes and volcanoes that occur in other parts of the world. That's because Australia is riding in the middle of a tectonic plate. Most volcanic and earthquake activity occurs along plate edges. It is at those edges that tremendous masses of rock may be rubbed together and heated into molten rock, called magma, which explodes out of volcanoes. The edge of the plate Australia rides on is slowly smashing into Asia, pushing up the

*Called Protesters' Falls, this lovely waterfall is part of
Nightcap National Park in New South Wales.*

tremendous Himalaya Mountains, which get taller every year. Another moving edge is producing volcanoes in New Zealand. Lava spurting out of volcanoes can harden, building up mountains, too. Yet Australia, in the middle of a tectonic plate, feels few of these effects. It has been quiet for about 100 million years. It once had mountains as high as the Himalayas, but these mountains were worn down long ago. Today Australia is very flat in comparison to other continents.

Take One Continent, Add Water

As continents go, Australia is fairly easy to figure out—once you know where the water is—because in this dry land, water can be the difference between life and death. Without water, crops can't grow. Without water, pasturelands dry out, and sheep and cattle die. Truck drivers bring huge jugs of water along on their trips in case their trucks break down. In the hot sun and dry air, that water could save their lives because a water source may be hundreds of miles away.

Green Strip of Land

Australia's water story begins at the ocean. On the east coast of Australia, western-blowing trade winds carry water vapor from the ocean, over the land. The mountains strip the rain from the winds. Here's how it happens: the air rises as it travels up the slopes of the Great Dividing Range. As air rises, it cools. Because cool air cannot hold as much water vapor as warm air, the water vapor forms raindrops, and rains down from the sky. This rainy area is green and fertile—good for crops in the lowlands. Pockets of rain forest blanket some of the hills. Waterfalls gush over mountains as small streams rush to the ocean. But the wind is very dry by the time it reaches the other side of the mountains.

Give a Sheep a Drink

The central eastern lowlands receive dry, rainless wind. Good thing this area has a hidden water source: the Great Artesian Basin. The Great Artesian Basin is an underground layer of rock that has holes filled with water. This underground water supply is fed by runoff from the eastern highlands that percolates down into porous rock, such as sandstone. The underground water flows under pressure, bubbling out of cracks in the ground called artesian springs. To reach this water, Australians have drilled more than nine thousand wells. The only problem is that the water is salty—too salty for people to drink or to use on crops. (Much of the water is also hot and smells like rotten eggs.) Sheep, however, can drink this water. So the land in this region supports millions of sheep. Just south of this basin is Australia's greatest river system, the Murray-Darling, which provides more water for cattle and growing crops.

NEW ZEALAND: AN ISLAND NATION

Many people think New Zealand and Australia are close together and very similar. Both were settled by the British and are now independent countries. But actually these two countries are quite far apart, not only in distance, but in climate and geology as well. New Zealand, a mountainous island, is 1,200 miles (1,935 kilometers) southeast of Australia. New Zealand is very geologically active, with many volcanoes, because it's on the edge of a tectonic plate.

In addition to active volcanoes, boiling hot springs, and bubbling mud pools, New Zealand has rushing rivers and green, productive countryside. Mild weather and plenty of rainfall make it a good place for growing fruit and raising sheep. Like Australia, New Zealand is one of the world's major exporters of wool, dairy products, and lamb. But otherwise, this green, lush mountainous land is far different from it's hot, flat, dry cousin, Australia.

DRY, DRY, DRY

Three-quarters of the continent, Australia's western plateau, is dry most of the time. Far from the ocean's moisture, it has little water. So it's made up of mostly semidesert or desert, such as the Great Sandy, the Gibson, and the Great Victorian deserts. These desert landscapes vary. Some are gibber deserts, meaning they are pebbly. Others are sandy, or solid rock. Many of these deserts have startlingly red dirt. The Simpson Desert contains the world's longest sand dunes, which run side-by-side for 124 miles (200 kilometers). In these deserts, it can be blistering hot during the day. (Marble Bar, in western Australia, experienced 162 consecutive days with temperatures over 100°F [38°C]!) But once the sun sets, it can be very chilly at night.

SEEING CONNECTIONS: SUN, SKIN, AND THE SOUTHERN EXPOSURE

In general, Australians have access to clean water, clean air, good food, and live long lives. But they also have the highest rate of skin cancer in the world. They can blame it partly on where they live. Skin cancer, which can be deadly, is caused mainly by exposure to the ultraviolet rays in sunlight. Because of its weather and its position on earth, Australia receives particularly high doses of ultraviolet rays.

Fortunately for humans and other animals, earth has a natural protection against these harmful rays. The ozone layer, a layer of ozone gas high up in the atmosphere, blocks some of these damaging rays. But in recent years, scientists have noticed that the ozone layer is thinning, especially in summer, over the North and South Poles. This may

The longest sand dunes in the world cover the surface of the Simpson Desert in Western Australia.

be part of an overall thinning of the ozone layer caused by human-made chemicals that destroy it. (Many ozone-destroying chemicals have been banned and are no longer used. But those used in the past continue to damage the ozone layer.)

Australia is near the thinned ozone layer that surrounds the South Pole. In the 1980s, scientists noticed that the ozone layer over Australia had thinned. This may be one reason why skin cancer rates have been so high among Australians. Other factors play a role as well. Australia has lots of sunny weather, and Australians tend to spend a lot of their free time outdoors: at the beach, playing outdoor sports, or just throwing some ribs

> **NATURAL DISASTERS**
>
> Australia may not be prone to earthquakes or volcanoes, but even so, it has natural disasters aplenty. The northern coast is vulnerable to cyclones, low-pressure atmospheric systems with swirling winds that bring heavy rains. (Hurricanes are very strong cyclones.) In 1974, Cyclone Tracy destroyed 12,000 houses and apartments in the city of Darwin. Flash floods, which occur when rivers fill quickly with water, are a risk in many parts of Australia, too.
>
> Because it is such a dry continent, Australia is also at risk from fires and dust storms. Fires can spread rapidly, racing as walls of flame across the land. During dry years, winds can whip up huge clouds that cover entire cities with dust. This dust can be very damaging, ruining machinery and making it difficult for people and other animals to breathe.

on the "barbie" (having a backyard barbecue). Tanning and sunning are popular activities, so Australians' exposure to the sun is very high. Ranchers, farmers, and other outdoor workers can get tremendous amounts of sun while working. In contrast to darker-skinned Australians, Australians of European descent, with white or pinkish skin, are particularly at risk for skin cancer. They have much less melanin—the natural skin pigment that helps protect humans from sunburn and skin cancer. Although they have a lower risk, dark-skinned people can still get skin cancer.

To combat the skin cancer problem, Australia's Public Health Association and other organizations are encouraging people to protect themselves from the sun. They have a "Slip, Slop, Slap" campaign that encourages people to slip on long-sleeved shirts, slop on sunscreen, and slap hats onto their heads, to protect themselves from the sun. This is one more way that Australians have adjusted to life in the Land Down Under.

Underground homes keep the residents of Coober Pedy cool. Despite the fact that they are very much like caves, these desert homes have the full range of modern conveniences.

THREE

THE NATURE OF AUSTRALIA

In Australia, you could climb into a misty rain forest and see parrots, frogs, and moss-laden trees. You could walk across a desert, hot and sunny, with ground like a strange pebbled street. You could gallop a horse through waving grasses, racing kangaroos hop-by-hop. Or you could swim in a school of rainbow-colored fish while a sea turtle paddles along. All this is possible because Australia contains a variety of biomes—areas with certain communities of animals and plants. These biomes include deserts, grasslands, savannas, woodlands, rain forests, coral reefs, and more.

MAPPING THE MOISTURE

If you look at a map of Australia's rainfall, you can more or less tell where the land biomes lie. The dry center of Australia, and the area slightly to the west, are desert or semidesert. Here the land is almost bare—sand dunes cover some places; others are pebbled like a dry streambed. In the semidesert, small shrubs grow scattered on red soil. Salt lakes, such as Lake Eyre, fill only after heavy rains. Most of the time these salt lakes are large, flat expanses covered with a crust of dried salt.

In these dry lands, which make up most of the land mass of Australia, plants are few and far between. This region receives less than 10 inches (25 centimeters) of rain, on average, each year. Yet when the rains do come, they change the land. Shield shrimp eggs, which lie dormant in the dirt during dry times, suddenly hatch, and the shrimp

> ### Frog for Your Throat
>
> If your throat is dry, and you are desperate for water, where do you find water in the dry lands of Australia? Aborigines have several traditional methods. Some plant roots contain moisture, if you squeeze them. You can also cut a branch of the mallee tree, make a hole in it, and drain the water it contains.
>
> But the most famous method is to find a water-holding frog. In a dry riverbed, stamp your foot on the ground, until a frog croaks in reply. Dig down and you'll find a water-holding frog. These frogs survive in burrows, inside special sacs filled with water from the last rains. Drinking the water from around the frog should quench your thirst. (This may sound gross, but it could save your life!) The frogs normally come out only during heavy rains, to eat, mate, and lay eggs in temporary rain-filled puddles. Then they dig back down into the ground to live in their water-filled sacs until it rains again.

wiggle in temporary puddles and pools. Millions of wildflowers sprout and bloom, carpeting the land with spectacular pinks, blues, yellows, and golds. So many wildflowers grow here that scientists are still discovering new ones.

The desert and semidesert regions of the Outback are hot during the day, but quickly cool at night. Animals such as hairy-nosed wombats, hopping mice, and kowaris—gerbil-like marsupials—beat the heat by hiding in burrows during the day and being active at night. Snakes and lizards are mostly nocturnal, or night-active, as well. Even people hide out from the heat—in Coober Pedy, a desert town, four out of ten people live in underground homes hollowed out like caves!

Great Grazers

Edging the desert and semidesert is an uneven border of grassland and savanna. Grassland, as you might guess, is covered with grass. There's not enough water for trees, except along streambeds. Savanna, a special type of grassland, is a little wetter, so it has widely spaced trees and shrubs, in addition to grass. This region gets approximately 10 to 30 inches (25 to 76 centimeters) of rainfall yearly.

Wherever there is grass, there are grazers (grass eaters): deer in Europe, llamas in South America, zebras in Africa. But Australia's grass eaters look very different from the four-legged, hoofed herd animals that graze on other continents. In southern Australia, large kangaroos and wallabies, which are small kangaroos, are the grazers. Emus, giant flightless birds that stand 6 feet (1.8 meters) tall, weigh 120 pounds (54 kilograms), and can run 30 miles (48 kilometers) per hour, graze on Australia's grasses as well. And in northern Australia, the main grazers are truly tiny: they're termites! Cone-shaped mud mounds, where these antlike insects live in colonies, rise up 6 or more feet (1.8 or more meters) and dot the landscape, mile after mile.

SMELL THE TREES: WOODLANDS

What's blue-green and smells like cough drops? Eucalyptus trees, Australia's most famous plants. More than 500 species of eucalyptus, also called gum trees, are native to Australia and nearby islands. With thick, tough leaves, these plants resist water loss. They can even turn their leaves sideways to avoid direct sunlight and its heat. Another water-saving, energy-saving feature is being evergreen. They drop their leaves only a few at a time—not all at once as many North American trees do in autumn. This means they only have to replace their leaves a few at a time. (Eucalyptus trees *do* shed their bark, which comes off in red, brown, or white flakes and curls over time.)

Eucalyptus trees are one of the major tree types you'll find in Australian woodlands, a kind of forest. Located at the edges of the grasslands and savannas, woodlands receive more rain than savannas but less than rain forests. Woodlands receive approximately 30 to 59 inches (76.9 to 151.3 centimeters) of rainfall each year. Woodlands are

Enormous termite mounds are part of the scenery at Kakadu National Park near the coastline of the Northern Territory.

home to frogs; huge fruit-eating bats called flying foxes; and birds such as parrots, lorikeets, and kookaburras. They're also home to many marsupials—mammals with pouches. One of these marsupials, a kind of possum called a squirrel glider, jumps off branches and glides from tree to tree on winglike skin flaps stretched between its arms and legs!

REMARKABLE RAIN FORESTS

Strangely enough, even the dry continent of Australia has rain forests. Rain forests receive more than 59 inches (150 centimeters) of rainfall yearly. They are tucked in the mountains of Australia's east coast and on Tasmania. Like North America, Australia contains two kinds of rain forests: temperate rain forests and tropical rain forests. Tropical rain forests are located in the tropics, closest to the equator. Temperate rain forests are in the temperate zone. Temperate rain forests have tall trees, lush green plants, ferns, and mossy tree trunks, like tropical rain forests. But they don't have the wide variety of species that tropical forests do.

Australia's tropical rain forests look a lot like tropical rain forests elsewhere. They have tall trees, many layers of plants, and colorful birds. But one thing is missing: monkeys. Instead, Australia's tropical rain forests are filled with a wide variety of possums, such as foxlike cuscuses, ringtail possums, and brushtail possums.

FIRE: FRIEND OR FOE?

A wildfire can be a fearsome thing. Fires in the Australian grasslands can sweep across the land with a wall of fire several miles long, burning seemingly everything in their path. Fire, however, is not always a disaster for wild species. Many plants are adapted to it. Some Australian plants, including the wildflower Banksia, need fire. The heat of the fire causes Banksia seedpods to open and drop seeds to the ground. Once the ash that covers the ground cools, it acts as a fertilizer, nourishing the seeds.

Other plants survive fire because they have deep underground root systems or thick protective bark. After a fire, these plants may send out new shoots. The new tender plant growth is good food for some animals. So fire may not be such a bad thing, after all.

Fire is natural, at least in some landscapes. Lightning has always sparked fires in Australia, especially during droughts, when plants are dry and quickly burn. Fires became even more common once humans came to Australia. Traditionally, Aborigines used a method called firestick farming. They set small controlled fires to provide a range of fresh plants and grasses that attracted animals they hunted.

This large arboreal (tree-dwelling) marsupial, a spotted cuscus, was photographed in the rain forest on Queensland's Cape York Peninsula.

One tropical rain forest dweller, the bowerbird, is a real interior decorator. The male bowerbird makes a nestlike stage, called a bower, out of twigs glued together with saliva. It carefully decorates the bower with berries, flowers, feathers, mosses, or anything else it finds, including shiny bottlecaps and foil! Some bowerbirds make paint by crushing berries, then spreading the paint on the bower walls with a slightly chewed twig—a paintbrush, of sorts. Once the bower is built, the male carries out a bobbing, hopping dance to attract a female, who inspects the bower. Males with the most elaborate bowers seem to be the most successful at finding mates.

Underwater Australia

Australia's Great Barrier Reef is so tremendous that astronauts can see it from outer space. This massive structure stretches 1,250 miles (2,000 kilometers), skirting Australia's northeastern coast. Despite its name, the Great Barrier Reef is made up of many smaller, separate reefs—2,500 or so. These reefs are bordered by the warm tropical waters of the Coral Sea.

Coral reefs, even the Great Barrier Reef, are made by tiny animals less than an inch long. These small, soft-bodied animals, called coral polyps, live in colonies and secrete limestone beneath them. This living layer of animals sits on the surface of a limestone mass—the reef—that they have made over hundreds of years. At night, the polyps extend tentacles to catch food in the surrounding water. But they get additional food from zooxanthellae, tiny algae that live inside their soft flesh.

If you like variety, you'll love the Great Barrier Reef. It has 400 kinds of coral, 1,500 species of fish, and 4,000 species of mollusks, which are sea snails and their relatives. Among the corals live giant clams, sea cucumbers, sea urchins, sea slugs, clown fish, damselfish, octopuses, sharks, rays, and a mind-boggling range of other sea life. Fortunately, Australians are well aware that their reef is a natural treasure. In 1983, the Australian government established a 135,000-square-mile (350,000-square-kilometer) national park that encompasses the Great Barrier Reef. Today this park, the Great Barrier Reef Marine Park, is the largest marine reserve in the world.

BETWEEN THE SEA AND THE SHORE

Many of the creatures that live in coral reefs start life in nearby mangroves and sea grass beds. Mangrove swamps are an in-between biome, a transition between ocean and land. Trees, called mangroves, grow there. Yet these trees are washed by rising and falling ocean tides. Mangrove trees are specially adapted for standing in water and handling shifting tides. They have special roots, called prop roots, that help hold them up. Other roots stick up from the mud, to gather oxygen. And young mangroves develop on long cigarlike roots that fall off the trees and float elsewhere, or stick in the mud and begin to grow. Among the roots of mangroves, small fish and crabs can begin life in a sheltered place.

Near the mangroves and reefs are sea grass beds, which are underwater pastures of aquatic grass. Of course, you won't find regular cows grazing these pastures. Instead, in Australia, you'll see "sea cows," also called dugongs—huge torpedo-shaped mammals with flippers and whalelike tails. A dugong can weigh 900 pounds (408.2 kilograms) and reach lengths of 11 feet (3.4 meters). Yet all dugongs eat is sea grass. Dugongs are relatives of manatees, sea mammals that live along the coast of Florida. In coastal waters, and in coastal rivers, you'll also find saltwater crocodiles, "salties." In the 1970s, salties were fairly rare, but limits on hunting them have helped the population bounce back. The only problem is that crocodile attacks on humans and cattle are on the rise.

OCTOPUS'S GARDEN

The Great Barrier Reef isn't the only mecca of marine life near Australia. On the southern fringes of the continent is an underwater offshore forest that's packed with seals, fish, and other sea life. This biome is the kelp forest. Anchored on the sea floor, the tremendous kelp plants reach up to the surface, like flexible trees. Air-filled floats called

Leafy sea dragons blend in well with their surroundings in the kelp forest along Australia's southern coast.

pneumatocysts hold up the plants, which may be 98 feet (30 meters) from bottom to top. (You think you have growth spurts? Kelp can grow up to a foot [31 centimeters] a day!) Like the kelp forests off California's coast, these forests are in the temperate zone.

Among Australian kelp's waving fronds live sea urchins, tube worms, sea spiders, sea slugs, mackerel, octopuses, fur seals, and blue-ringed octopuses. The tiny 8-inch (20-centimeter) blue-ringed octopus is one of most poisonous creatures on earth. Fortunately, it usually eats just crabs and fish. But its venom can be lethal to humans. Another famous kelp dweller is the leafy sea dragon, a relative of the sea horse. Like sea horses, leafy sea dragons resemble the seaweed where they hide; they're also some of the few male animals that get pregnant. A male sea dragon, which is about a foot (31 centimeters) long, inflates a large pouch on its body in order to attract a female, which lays her eggs inside the pouch. Five weeks later, one hundred or more young sea dragons are born, squeezed out of the male's belly pouch!

PRESERVING BIOMES: WHAT'S NATURAL AND WHAT'S NOT?

If you were managing a natural park and lightning started a fire, would you let that fire burn down a forest? Would you kill kangaroos if there were so many that they were eating endangered plants? What if huge starfish were consuming coral, leaving a dead coral reef behind? Would you remove the starfish, or let nature take its course? These are the kinds of decisions park managers must make on a regular basis. Natural parks and wildlife refuges are set aside to preserve samples of deserts, forests, grasslands, coral reefs, and other biomes. People want to keep these places natural. But in Australia, as elsewhere, it's often hard to decide exactly what is natural and what is not.

Even without people around, biomes naturally change. Lightning-sparked fires burn grasslands. Trees sprout in grasslands, turning them into forests. Over time, climates become colder, or warmer, causing plants and animals to move to new areas or sometimes to die out.

No Swimming, No Joke!

If you're in Australia and you see a sign that says NO SWIMMING, take that sign very seriously. If you don't, you may dive into an ocean with sharks, a bay with jellyfish, or a river with alligators. Swimming, snorkeling, and scuba diving along Australian coasts and inland waters is often safe. But alligator attacks, though rare, can be deadly. So stay away from waters they frequent. Shark attacks are uncommon, too, mostly because huge shark nets strung offshore keep sharks from coming into designated swimming areas along beaches.

Perhaps the most dangerous aquatic animal is a type of jellyfish. In parts of northern Australia—but not the Great Barrier Reef—swimmers occasionally encounter box jellyfish. These jellyfish, also called sea wasps, can have tentacles 15 feet (4.6 meters) long. A box jellyfish's stings are not always deadly. But if you get enough of its sixty tentacles wrapped around you, it can kill you within four minutes. To avoid being stung, it's best not to swim in northern Australian waters in seasons when box jellyfish are numerous. Some people who do swim in these waters wear pantyhose to protect themselves. Not only do these swimmers wear pantyhose on their legs, they slip another pair on their arms, as well. The nylon material helps prevent jellyfish stingers from penetrating the swimmer's skin.

Aborigines: People in the Picture

In Australia, people are a fairly recent arrival. Between 40,000 and 100,000 years ago, Aborigines migrated from southeast Asia to Australia. They may have walked across land bridges—pieces of land that once bridged parts of the sea separating Australia and Asia. They may have used rafts to cross the remaining waters in between.

Once they arrived, Aborigines lived more or less in harmony with the land. Over the years, they learned which plants to eat. They moved from place to place, hunting kangaroos and other animals. They developed a complex culture, intricate folklore, and a deep, spiritual connection to the land.

Aborigines did not build permanent homes or till the soil or change the land in obvious ways. But two of their practices—hunting animals and setting fires—have affected Australian biomes forever. The role of fire is perhaps the easiest to examine. Aborigines set fires in order to provide fresh green plants to attract animals to hunt. Setting fires created a patchwork landscape of forest, field, and shrub, where many animals lived and many edible plants grew. Scientists believe that over the last 40,000 years this practice, called firestick farming, has changed the landscape of Australia, giving fire-adapted plants and animals a survival advantage. These days, when people do not set controlled fires regularly, as the Aborigines did, some Australian animals actually decline! For example, malas, which are small kangaroos that live near Uluru, decreased in number after Aborigines were removed from the land by the Australian government. Part of the reason for their decline may have been because the Aborigines were no longer there to set fires.

Dance is an important part of aboriginal culture. Elders (in the background) pass their heritage on to their children.

THE FIRST AUSTRALIANS

For forty thousand years, Australia's only human inhabitants were the Aborigines. They spoke four hundred or more languages and had a complex culture. Their sacred songs and stories, told to one another generation after generation, were connected to physical features of the landscape, along paths called songlines. Full of spiritual meaning, these stories also gave each Aborigine a mental map of physical features of Australia and knowledge of mountains, valleys, boulders and outcrops, even ones they had never visited personally. Aborigines created the largest art gallery in the world, made up of petroglyphs—beautiful paintings on rocks—that cover boulders for hundreds of miles. The paintings depict handprints, animals, and boomerangs—hunting tools used by the Aborigines. Some of the paintings appear to be thousands of years old.

Australia is now populated by people from all over the world. The British, who landed in 1788, were the first settlers after the Aborigines. When the British arrived, about three hundred thousand Aborigines lived undisturbed on the land. Disease brought by newcomers, as well as fatalities in bloody conflicts, decreased the numbers of Aborigines drastically. Today, there are approximately one hundred and fifty thousand Aborigines living in Australia. Like Native Americans in the United States, Aborigines control special reserves—areas of land set aside for them. Some chose to live on these reserves; other Aborigines live elsewhere. Most live modern lives and use modern technologies; but some also try to preserve their traditional culture and hunting practices. The Aborigines, who have been discriminated against in the past, continue to fight for their rights.

How hunting has changed Australia's landscape is more complex and controversial. After the Aborigines arrived in Australia many large animals, such as giant kangaroos and huge flightless birds (larger than emus), died out. Did the Aborigines kill them off through hunting? Or did the climate change, making conditions unfavorable for the survival of these animals? No one is sure of the answer. But these animals may have become extinct as a result of a combination of climate change, hunting, and firestick farming.

The challenge for park managers today is to preserve the species that exist now. Parts of the Australian landscape are fire-adapted, shaped by Aboriginal firestick farming over time. So park workers occasionally set fires, as the Aborigines did. Park managers strive to maintain healthy biomes, with a balance of animal and plant species, that reflect the diversity and history of Australia.

The kangaroo is one of the national symbols of Australia, which is home to about fifty different kangaroo species.

FOUR

MARVELOUS MARSUPIALS AND MONOTREMES

Could you go for seventeen years without drinking any water? Can you jump 33 feet (10 meters) in one big hop? When you were a baby, did your mother carry you around in a great big pocket? If so, then you have characteristics in common with some of Australia's marsupial species.

Marsupials are a kind of mammal. Mammals are warm blooded, have body hair or fur, and feed their babies milk through mammary glands. You are a mammal. So are horses, cats, dogs, cows, goats, moles, voles, chipmunks, lions, tigers, bears, mice, and whales! Australia's marsupials include kangaroos, koalas, wombats, and kangaroos.

MARSUPIALS: IT'S IN THEIR POCKETS!

Three features make marsupials different from other mammals such as people and cats. First, pregnant marsupials don't have a placenta. A placenta is the artery-filled organ that connects a mother and her fetus—her developing offspring. This organ regulates the exchange of food, oxygen, and wastes between mother and fetus during pregnancy. Second, unlike other mammals, marsupials give birth to young that are still not fully formed. At birth, a baby marsupial is blind and hairless, with little nubs for limbs and a body less than $1/2$ inch (1.3 centimeters) long. It pulls its way through its mother's fur and into her pouch. This pouch, where the mother carries the young after it is born, is the third difference between marsupials and other mammals. (The word *marsupial* comes from the Latin word *marsupium*, which means pouch or purse.) Most of the

Brushtail possums are marsupials found in Australia. Here, a baby approaches its mother's pouch.

world's 150 or so kinds of marsupials live in Australia. A few, such as opossums, are found on other continents.

Cool Kangaroos

When most people think of kangaroos, or "'roos," they imagine red kangaroos: long tailed, big as a person, hopping across dry bushlands. Kangaroos, however, come in many sizes and species. The dusky hopping mouse, a kangaroo, is as small as a mouse—just 2 inches (5 centimeters) tall. The largest kangaroos, male red kangaroos, are as tall as some basketball players, standing 6.6 feet (2 meters) and weighing 200 pounds (91 kilograms)! Some kangaroos travel in herds in the desert or climb like monkeys in rain-forest trees. Other kangaroo species resemble tiny bears or scruffy rats. Still others look like furry cats, or lanky kids playing hopscotch. Wallabies, bettongs, and potoroos are kinds of kangaroos, too. Australia contains somewhere around fifty kangaroo species; scientists cannot agree on an exact number.

Hop to It   What big feet kangaroos have! These feet, an enlarged fourth toe, and their powerful hind legs allow male red kangaroos to move as far as 33 feet (10 meters) in one hop. Red kangaroos, hopping quickly, travel 15 to 25 miles (24 to 40 kilometers) per hour. But in an emergency they can hop, for a short distance, at almost 40 miles (60 kilometers) per hour. A kangaroo's large tail acts as a counterbalance, pumping up and down as it hops. The tail also props it up when it is sitting. A kangaroo can also walk, using its tail as an extra leg; but hopping takes less energy.

Beat the Heat   Red kangaroos, and many other kangaroos, are well adapted to living in the hot bushlands of Australia. Groups of red kangaroos, called mobs, graze on grasses and shrubs in the dry plains. Mobs live close to water, within 10 to 15 miles (16.1 to 24.2 kilometers), and spend most of their day resting. That saves energy in the heat. Kangaroos have a low metabolic rate, meaning that they burn surprisingly little energy and, therefore, need less food and water. Even in the hot Australian summer, red kangaroos drink only about once a week. They need much less water than sheep, which drink about twice a day.

Kangaroos keep cool by lying in the shade. Their thick fur helps keep out some of the heat. Sweating when exercising, and panting like dogs when resting, helps cool them

Athough they may not look it, both this mouselike creature and this tree-climber are kangaroos.

off, too. Last but not least, kangaroos lick their forearms. That may sound strange, but it's another way of cooling themselves. Tiny blood vessels bring blood very close to the surface in kangaroos' forearms. When the saliva evaporates, it uses up heat energy from the kangaroos' body. This process of losing heat by evaporation is called evaporative cooling. Evaporative cooling is the reason why sweating and panting also work to cool the body.

WONDERFUL WOMBATS

At one time, wombats the size of cows wandered Australia, munching plants. Today, about thirty thousand years later, descendants of these wombats still munch plants but weigh only 60 to 100 pounds (26.8 to 45.4 kilograms) and burrow in the ground. With short legs and stocky, barrel-like bodies, these marsupials are built for burrowing. Their wide feet and long claws help them dig as much as 2 to 3 feet (61 to 91 centimeters) of tunnel in a night. The main predators of wombats are people and dingoes—wild dogs. But wombats are not an easy catch. They scramble to their burrows to escape, wedging themselves into their tunnels. Following a wombat into its tunnel can be hazardous. You wouldn't want its sharp teeth to sink into your skin. A wombat can also smother a predator, smashing it into a dead-end tunnel, where it eventually runs out of air. One scientist who tried to capture a wombat in a tunnel regretted it. The wombat temporarily pinned the scientist's hand to the wall!

A wombat leaves its burrow at night to feed, avoiding the daytime heat.

Both deserts and bushlands are home to wombats. Like many animals that live in hot climates, wombats are nocturnal. It's cooler at night, so the wombat does not risk losing water by sweating to cool off in the heat of the day. During the day, wombats stay in their burrows. Like a basement, an underground burrow stays cool even when the temperature soars outside.

Wombats are adapted for dry climates in another way, too. Super-efficient kidneys allow wombats to process waste without losing much water as urine. Because of this and other physical adaptations, these animals can survive as long as seventeen years without taking a drink of water!

Not So Cuddly Koalas

Koalas look so cute that it is tempting to pet them. But that may not be a good idea. Koalas are animals that spend most of their time alone. They seem to prefer solitude. If you try to pet a wild one, it may bite you or pee on you. Cuddling apparently stresses out most koalas. (And by the way, the proper name is koala, not koala bear. These animals are not bears at all!)

These sleepy, slow-moving animals, the national symbol of Australia, are active at night. They sleep eighteen hours a day. When they are awake, most of their time is spent up in trees, feeding on eucalyptus leaves. Near feeding koalas the air can smell like cough

---

The Tasmanian Devil

You've probably seen a cartoon character called the Tasmanian Devil. But did you know that there are real Tasmanian devils? They live on Tasmania, an island off the southeast coast of Australia. A real Tasmanian devil is about 12 inches (30 centimeters) high at the shoulder and weighs 25 pounds (11 kilograms)—making it about the size of a small dog. It is a marsupial. Although it occasionally hunts small birds and crayfish, the Tasmanian devil is mostly a scavenger—usually eating only animals that it finds already dead.

Tasmanian devils once lived on mainland Australia. But they disappeared from the mainland, perhaps because of competition from dingoes, wild dogs that were introduced from southeast Asia. As recently as six hundred years ago, there were still Tasmanian devils on mainland Australia. Now, Tasmanian devils live only on Tasmania, where there are no dingoes.

drops. That's because eucalyptus leaves are the source of eucalyptus oil, used in some cough drops. Yet these leaves also contain very toxic chemicals. Scientists still do not understand how koalas can eat such huge quantities of eucalyptus leaves without becoming sick.

Adult koalas have gray fur, large heads with round, hairy ears and black noses, and claws on their toes. They weigh about 20 pounds (9 kilograms), with the males being larger than the females. In the 1880s, koalas were killed by the thousands so that their fur could be used for clothing in Europe. But today, trapping and killing koalas is illegal. That has helped the koalas, but still their population is small. The primary reason for this is habitat loss—the cutting of the trees koalas need to eat. They eat the leaves of only a few species of eucalyptus trees, a very specialized diet. If those trees die out, koalas will, too.

Monotremes: They're Eggceptional!

Most of the world's mammals, including marsupials, give birth to live babies. But two Australian mammal species—the platypus and the echidna—lay eggs, instead. These egg layers are called monotremes. Monotremes are found only in New Guinea, mainland Australia, and the island of Tasmania.

The Peculiar Platypus

Duck-billed platypuses are mammals. But these cat-sized furry animals lay large-yolked leathery eggs, like a snake's eggs. They are the only mammals that are poisonous. (A spur, or clawlike bump, on the males' back legs contains enough venom to kill a dog.) Strangest of all, a platypus has a bill that looks a little like a duck's bill. But a platypus's bill is not really like a duck's, after all. The differences between the two became clear once a scientific mystery was solved in 1986.

Platypuses swim in lakes and deep pools of streams in Tasmania and on the east and southeast coast of Australia. They use their rubbery, flexible bills like sieves, to strain freshwater shrimp, worms, and insect larvae out of mud and sand. But what has always puzzled scientists about platypuses is that they close their eyes, ears, and nostrils when feeding underwater. So how do these animals find their food? Why don't they bump into rocks underwater? Until 1986, no one had the answers to those questions.

That year, scientists discovered that a platypus's bill detects electrical signals. It can even detect the electrical signals emitted by the muscles and nerves in the tail of a shrimp! The flow of water in a stream creates an electric field (a web of electrical charges), so any movement or directional changes, such as those caused by a rock underwater, can be detected by a platypus, too. This system is even more sophisticated than the electrical detection system used by sharks.

Platypuses keep their eyes closed underwater, and use an electrical detection system to find their prey.

Researchers still have much to learn about these surprising animals. But because platypuses are shy, difficult to find, and active only during evening hours, they are very hard to study.

ECCENTRIC ECHIDNA

Echidnas are small, spiny, ant-eating animals, about the size of a guinea pig. Their 6-inch- (15-centimeter-) long tongues, covered with sticky saliva, are perfect for licking up ants and termites, which are the echidnas' major meals. When disturbed, an echidna curls up in a ball, covering its vulnerable head and belly. (Only dingoes occasionally eat an echidna; no other animal makes a meal of this spiny mouthful.) Although the young echidna hatches out of an egg, it spends the next three months in its mother's pouch, where it drinks milk. The short-beaked echidna lives in Australia; the long-beaked echidna lives in Papua New Guinea.

An echidna can quickly roll itself into a spine-covered ball to protect its head and belly, which have no spines.

WHY ARE AUSTRALIAN ANIMALS SO UNIQUE?

You won't find a wild kangaroo on a European grassland or a platypus in an American pond. These and many other animals are found only in Australia and on nearby islands. That means they are endemic, found nowhere else on earth. Why does Australia have so many unique animals? The answer lies in the continent's history.

Australia's animals and plants are unique because the Australian continent has been isolated from other landmasses for so long. About 150 million years ago, Australia was part of Gondwana, the southern half that had broken off from Pangaea, the first big supercontinent. Gondwana included Africa, South America, Antarctica, India, and the Arabian Peninsula. These connected landmasses had many animals and plants in common because animals could fly, swim, and walk from one to another. Seeds, floating in water, flying through the air, or carried in animals' feces or fur, spread among the continents as well. But then, as the earth's tectonic plates shifted and the sea floor spread out, Australia and Antarctica moved away from the other landmasses. Eventually, sixty-five million years ago, Australia broke off on its own.

Since the time when it was part of Gondwana, Australia's climate has changed. It has become very dry. A sea that once filled its center has disappeared. Its tremendous mountains have worn down. Many animal and plant species have died out. But some have survived. Over millions of years, Australia's animals and plants have adapted to the "new" Australia. From sixty-five million years ago until modern times, very few animals made the journey to Australia from neighboring continents such as Asia. So, many Australian land animals and land plants evolved on their own, without competition from animals and plants from other continents. In their own little corner of the earth, Australian animals and plants evolved into the strange, wonderful, unique species we see today.

Australians have tried to rid their land of rabbits in numerous ways. Flushing rabbits out of their holes and netting them is one method, but such attempts do not cause a significant decrease in the rabbit population.

FIVE

THE RABBIT THAT ALMOST ATE AUSTRALIA . . . AND OTHER ANIMAL ISSUES

As on every continent where humans live, Australia has the typical environmental problems associated with modern life: air pollution, water pollution, land pollution, overdevelopment, and loss of animal habitat. But Australia also has environmental issues that are uniquely Australian in nature. These issues have to do with animals—large numbers of animals—rabbits, toads, kangaroos, sheep, dogs, and more. People differ in their views on how best to control these animal populations and where these animals belong.

RABBITS, RABBITS, AND MORE RABBITS

When Easter comes around, some Australians don't celebrate with Easter bunnies. They buy chocolate Easter bilbys instead. Bilbys, which are rabbitlike marsupials, are native to Australia. They are also one of the many Australian species in danger of becoming extinct. The bilby's number-one enemy is the European wild rabbit, so it's no wonder Easter bunnies aren't popular with everyone. Rabbits, which aren't native to Australia, eat the same foods bilbys do and use the same burrows bilbys need. In the last century, twenty-three native mammal species, including one species of bilby, have died out—in large part, because of rabbits and foxes. Both rabbits and foxes were brought to Australia by English settlers who wanted to use them in sport hunting.

BREEDING LIKE RABBITS

The rabbit "takeover" of Australia started small. In 1859, Thomas Austin released twenty-four wild European rabbits on his Australian ranch in southern Victoria. Seven years later, he and his fellow sportsmen were able to shoot an amazing 14,253 rabbits on his property. Obviously, the rabbit's reputation for producing lots of offspring is well deserved! Rabbits spread like a plague over the countryside. Austin and the other sportsmen who brought rabbits to Australia soon had more than they'd bargained for.

Millions of Munchers

Just how much damage can furry little bunnies do? Plenty, if there are hundreds of millions of them. Farmers saw their crops destroyed by the hungry rabbits. In places, sheep and cattle went hungry because the rabbits had eaten almost all the plants! It takes only about sixteen rabbits to eat as much grass as one sheep does. So the economic damage done by rabbits has been tremendous. According to official estimates, rabbits have caused ranchers to lose as much as $75 million in wool and beef revenues in a single year.

Native Animals Lose Out

By competing for food and burrows, rabbits cause trouble for native animals such as bilbys and burrowing bettongs. Furthermore, because the rabbits have become so numerous, the population of foxes and feral cats, which eat rabbits, has increased. Unfortunately, these foxes and cats kill bilbys and burrowing bettongs, too. What has made matters worse is that programs to poison, trap, and kill rabbits have also killed native mammals such as rat-kangaroos and tiger-cats.

Soil Under Siege

Rabbits also damage the land. Hordes of hungry rabbits eat grasses and tender plants, leaving woody shrubs behind. They eat tree bark, killing trees. After the rabbits are finished with an area, there are few plants left to hold the soil in place. As a result, during drought years, the soil may dry out and blow away, turning productive grassland and savanna into unproductive desert.

The War on Rabbits

To stop the spread of rabbits, people in Australia have tried hunting, trapping, and poisoning them. They have built fences to keep the rabbits from spreading. But the rabbits still come back. At times, so many rabbits have piled up on top of each other that the last rabbits have been able to scramble over the bodies of other rabbits and hop over the fences! One researcher has estimated you could kill off 70 percent of Australia's rabbits in a single year, but by the next year the population would have rebounded to its previous size.

In the 1950s, to control the rabbit populations, scientists in Australia infected them with myxomatosis, a deadly rabbit disease. The disease killed 500 million of the 600 million rabbits in Australia at that time. But the success of the myxomatosis

> ### THE WORLD'S BIGGEST FENCE
>
> What's 6 feet (1.8 meters) high, 3,700 miles (5,970 kilometers) long, and full of holes? The Wild Dog Fence of Australia. This fence, the world's largest, is longer than the Great Wall of China! The Wild Dog Fence, which people began building in the 1880s, stretches across the southeastern corner of Australia, winding its way through South Australia, New South Wales, and Queensland. The purpose of the fence is to keep dingoes, the yellowish wild dogs of Australia, out of the south, which is prime grazing land for sheep. The wild dogs hunt and kill sheep, in addition to native animals.
>
> Wool is a major export for Australia, so ranchers believe that the millions of dollars spent to repair the fence are worth investing. But the fence is full of holes. Animals dig under the fence and tear through it. The fence is difficult and expensive to monitor and repair. How well it works is questionable. Should it be maintained? On this particular issue, there really are people on both sides of the fence!

project was short lived. Over the next few generations of rabbits, some rabbits built up a resistance to the disease and began surviving the infection. As of 1996, there were still 200 to 300 million rabbits on the loose in Australia.

Scientists began studying a new disease, rabbit calcivirus disease, in the 1990s. Researchers started experimenting with the virus in 1995, carefully controlling it by infecting only rabbits kept in pens on Wardang Island, near South Australia. But somehow the virus accidentally spread off the island and onto mainland Australia. Rabbit calcivirus disease is now sweeping through rabbit populations. Will this virus solve the rabbit problem? No one knows. It is unclear how the uncontrolled spread of this virus will affect the rabbit population overall. Research indicates the virus doesn't normally spread to other wild animals or people. But a few scientists are concerned that the spreading virus could mutate—genetically change—and affect other kinds of animals, too. Only time will tell.

PLANTS AND ANIMALS OUT OF PLACE

When people move to a new country, they often like to bring familiar plants and animals with them. Dingoes, the wild dogs of Australia, are the descendants of domestic dogs brought to Australia by people from southeast Asia about four thousand years ago. In the last two centuries, Europeans have introduced not just rabbits but also scores of other exotic (non-native) animals and plants to Australia. Cats were brought for companions . . . and perhaps to kill mice, another import. Cows were brought for milk and meat. People also brought flowers, trees, buffalo, sheep, and pigs. There were species people brought accidentally, too, such as rats that crawled inside ships' cargo in one port and escaped when they reached another—in Australia.

Of the species that are brought to a new country, some die. Others survive but don't spread beyond gardens and pastures. Still others disperse widely, becoming pests. Why do plants and animals that were no problem in their home country suddenly spread far and wide in a new location? Often it's because they have a survival advantage in their new habitat. In their home country, they, along with the plants and animals around them, have evolved side by side over thousands of years. Usually there are animals that eat them or plants that compete with them. Plants and animals develop defenses against one another. But in the new environment, there may not be any naturally occurring predators or competitors to keep the population of exotic species in check.

Killer Plants

Exotic plants are a big threat to Australian species. Rubber vine, an exotic that entangles trees and other plants, is spreading quickly along Australian rivers, killing off native plants. More than four hundred exotic plants have been tested as pasture grasses to feed cows and sheep. Unfortunately, only a few became useful pasture grasses. Yet forty of the experimental species have spread, becoming problem weeds. One, para grass, is choking the wetlands of Kakadu National Park, in the Northern Territories.

Dangerous Dumping

Exotic species can threaten aquatic species, too. Seventy or so exotic species live in Australia's rivers and coastal waters. Many of these came to Australia in ballast water—water that was pumped into an empty ship's hull to increase its weight and balance it. Tremendous amounts of the water may be carried as ballast from one port and released in another. Today scientists are concerned about starfish that recently came to Australia in ballast water from Japan. These starfish may eat many of the ocean animals on Australia's southern coast.

Kitties Gone Wild

Even domestic animals such as cats, dogs, pigs, horses, and goats can cause problems for wild animals. Stray domestic animals can become feral, reproducing in the wild and competing with native animals for food and space. Pigs and buffalo, for instance, are destroying wildlife habitat in some Australian parks by eating the plants and churning up the soil with their hooves.

Terrible Toads

Often people import animals with the best of motives. In 1935, Australian sugarcane growers had a problem. Grubs—fat, caterpillar-like larvae—were eating their crops. They came up with a clever solution: import grub-eating toads! Cane toads, which are native to Central America, are almost 10 inches (25 centimeters) long and can weigh 4 pounds (1.8 kilograms). The solution seemed terrific. So Australians brought grub-gobbling toads into the country. But the plan backfired terribly. Now residents of eastern Queensland and New South Wales wish the toads would just go home.

The toads have not stayed in the cane fields; they seem to prefer other habitats and have spread throughout the countryside. Sometimes the toads are so plentiful they dot people's yards, one every few feet. These big hoppers gobble not just grubs but all kinds of insects, including honeybees. They'll even feed out of a dog's bowl. In addition, the toads are very poisonous, so dogs and cats that try to eat them can die. If a toad gets into a water source for cattle, the cows that drink the water get sick. Trying to make the best of things, Australians have started businesses to make the toads' skin into leather. They also export some toads for school study and laboratory research.

Sheep, Cows, Crops, and Kangaroos

English settlers arrived in Australia in 1788. Since then these and other immigrants have changed the Australian landscape. They have cut down forests, cleared land for pastures, planted crops, drilled wells for water, dammed rivers, and established ranches and farms. These changes have harmed many Australian mammals, such as small kangaroos. But the changes have helped some animals, too.

Large kangaroos—eastern gray kangaroos, western gray kangaroos, red kangaroos, wallaroos, and whiptail wallabies—have all increased in number over the years. Just like deer in North America, large kangaroos have benefited from people's changes to the landscape. These large kangaroos are grazers, so they can use the pastures people create. They can also drink from water holes made for cows. The problem is that there are so many kangaroos that they are eating crops, damaging fences, and consuming the food and water needed by sheep and cattle.

Could You Shoot a 'Roo?

Unlike rabbits, foxes, and cane toads, kangaroos are native animals. They belong in Australia. But are there too many? Many farmers, ranchers, biologists, and even environmentalists say yes. As a result, kangaroos are shot and killed during regulated, licensed hunts each year. Kangaroos harvested in this way are used for their meat and skin. Animal rights activists have protested against the kangaroo hunts. But so far no practical alternative has been found.

A sign warns motorists to beware of kangaroos crossing the road. The dramatic increase of the kangaroo population has created problems in the Land Down Under.

KANGAROO BURGERS

Some people, in fact, are in favor of raising kangaroos deliberately, instead of cows. It may make sense. Kangaroos are adapted to the environment of Australia. Their soft hooves do not damage the soil as those of cattle and sheep do. In some areas, especially in dry years, cattle and sheep overgraze the land, churning up the soil with their hooves, leaving dried out, damaged, unproductive land. But could kangaroo meat and hide be as commercially successful as cow meat (beef) and hide? That question remains.

Australia Looks Toward the Future

Australia definitely has some intriguing animal dilemmas. But it's a mistake to blame every problem and every lost farm and ranch profit on rabbits, kangaroos, or dingoes. Australia is a land undergoing tremendous change. In the last two hundred years Europeans have tried to convert this dry land of the kangaroos into fertile farmland and pastureland for cattle and sheep. The natural biomes, the plant and animal communities Aborigines had learned to work with over tens of thousands of years, have been rapidly and drastically altered.

The rise and fall of animal populations may be, in some cases, only the most visible sign of deeper changes—changes in Australia's land use, soil condition, climate, and plant community. The need to understand Australia's environment, and plan for better land use in the future, is a challenge Australians are taking to heart.

GLOSSARY

Aborigines the first people in Australia, who arrived there from southeast Asia at least forty thousand years ago

biome an area that has a certain kind of climate and a certain kind of community of animals and plants

continent one of the seven great masses of land on the earth

desert a biome that receives less than 10 inches (25 centimeters) of precipitation each year

drought a long period without precipitation

endemic found in a certain region and nowhere else

equator the imaginary line that runs around the earth's middle

exotic species species that are not native to a region

feral term for an animal that was once domestic but is now living in the wild

firestick farming the Aboriginal farming method that involves setting small, controlled fires so that fresh grass and useful plants grow back on burned-over areas. This practice provides the tender plants and fresh grass that attract animals the Aborigines hunt.

grazer an animal that feeds on plants, such as grasses, that are not woody. (Bushes and trees, which are woody, are eaten by plant eaters called browsers.)

latitude a measure of distance, north or south, relative to the earth's equator

mammal any of a class of warm-blooded vertebrates—animals with backbones—that have body hair and secrete milk, generally through mammary glands

mammary glands   milk-producing glands found in mammals

mangrove swamp   a coastal wetland that contains mangrove trees

marsupial   a mammal that has a short gestation period, young that are only partly developed at birth, and a protective pouch for carrying its young

monotreme   a mammal that lays eggs and has some bone structures more similar to reptiles than mammals

Outback   the dry desert and semidesert regions of Australia

Pangaea   the original landmass (or supercontinent) that existed 250 million years ago, when the separate continents we know today were all joined together

Panthalassa   the ocean that surrounded Pangaea

savanna   a type of grassland that has widely spaced trees

semidesert   a biome that receives more precipitation than a desert, but not as much as a grassland, and is marked by widely spaced shrubby vegetation

supercontinent   a gigantic continent (Pangaea) that existed long ago, which later broke up to form the smaller continents we know today

tectonic plate   a large piece of the earth's crust that slides over molten rock below, gradually shifting its position on the earth's surface

tropical rain forest   a forest biome found in the tropics and characterized by warmth, very heavy rainfall, and high species diversity

woodland   a type of vegetation that has trees widely spread apart, usually not as close together as those of a forest. (A forest, in contrast, has trees that are close enough together to form a continuous canopy.)

FURTHER READING

BOOKS
(Books geared specifically to young people are marked with an asterisk.)

*Arnold, Caroline. *A Walk on the Great Barrier Reef*. Minneapolis: Carolrhoda, 1988.

Domico, Terry. *Kangaroos: The Marvelous Mob*. New York: Facts on File, 1993.

Evans, Howard Ensign, and Mary Alice Evans. *Australia, A Natural History*. Washington, D.C.: Smithsonian Institution, 1983.

*Garrett, Dan, and Warrill Grindrod. *Australia*. New York: Macmillan, 1989.

*Johnson, Rebecca L. *The Great Barrier Reef: A Living Laboratory*. Minneapolis: Lerner, 1991.

MacDougall, J. D. *A Short History of Planet Earth*. New York: John Wiley & Sons, 1996.

Morrison, Reg and Maggie Morrison. *Australia: The Four Billion Year Journey of a Continent*. New York: Facts on File, 1990.

Phillips, Ken. *Koalas: Australia's Ancient Ones*. New York: Macmillan, 1994.

Pine, Stephen J. *Burning Bush: A Fire History of Australia*. New York: Henry Holt, 1991.

*Ruiz de Larramendi, Alberto. *Australia: Land of Natural Wonders*. Chicago: Children's Press, 1994.

SELECTED ARTICLES ABOUT AUSTRALIA

International Wildlife

Alper, Joseph, and Susan Walton, "Dingoes on the Run." July/August 1990, 5–11.

Hoffman, Eric, "Paradox of the Platypus." January/February 1990, 18–21.

Montgomery, Sy, "Digging Is Their Game" [wombats]. March/April 1989, 47–50.

Underwood, Anne, "Where Have All the Malas Gone?" March/April 1995, 16–21.

National Geographic

Ellis, William S., "Queensland: Broad Shoulder of Australia." January 1986, 8–37.

Hamner, William M., "Australia's Box Jellyfish: A Killer Down Under." August 1994, 116–129.

Levathes, Louise E., "The Land Where the Murray Flows." August 1985, 252–278.

National Geographic Editors, "Travelers Look at Australia" [an insert map of Australia]. Special issue on Australia, February 1988.

Newman, Cathy, "The Uneasy Magic of Australia's Cape York Peninsula." June 1996, 2–46.

Payne, Oliver, "Koalas—Out on a Limb." April 1995, 36–59.

Natural History

Barboza, Perry S., "The Wombat Digs In." December 1995, 26–29.

Dawson, Terry, "Kangaroos, the Kings of Cool." April 1995, 39–44.

Flannery, Timothy, "Arrival of the Easter Bilby." April 1996, 16–17.

New Scientist

Anderson, Ian, "Sixth Sense Is the Platypus's Secret." May 12, 1988, 39.

Smithsonian

Domico, Terry, "The Faster a 'Roo Travels, the More Energy It Saves." November 1993, 102–108.

WORLD WIDE WEB

Australians are among the heaviest users of the Internet and the World Wide Web. It helps those living in isolated areas connect with the rest of the world. For information on Australia, you can search for articles on Australian animals and other Australian topics. The following Web site is a good starting point for research on the continent, its animals, and environmental issues:

Australian Environment On-line

http://www.erin.gov.au/

INDEX

Page numbers in ***boldface italics*** refer to illustrations.

Aborigines, 16, 30, 35–37, ***36***
Africa, 5, 46
alligators, 35
animals, 9–10, 28, 39–54
Antarctica, 5, 7, 46, 47
Antarctic Circle, 14
Arabian Peninsula, 46
Arctic Circle, 14
artesian springs, 21
Asia, 5, 7, 19
Austin, Thomas, 49–50
Australia, 5, 7
   animals, 9–10, 28, 39–54
   biomes, 27–35, 55
   cities, 9, 10
   climate, 9, 10, 13, 14, 21, 23, ***32***, 47
   deserts, 23, ***24***, 27–28
   geographic regions, 15
   geology, 19, 21
   lakes, 18, ***19***, 27
   minerals, 18
   mountains, 10, 15, ***16***
   natural disasters, 25
   Outback, 9, 10, 15, 28
   population, 10
   rainfall, 14, 18, 21, 27, 29, 30
   rivers, 18–19, 21
   seasons, 14
   states and territories, 10
   statistics and records within, 11
   terrain, ***22***
   world records held by, 11
Australian Capital Territory, 10
axis of earth, 15

bauxite, 18
bilbys, 49
biomes, 27–35, 55
birds, 30, 31
Blue Lake, 18
bowerbirds, 31
Bungle Bungles, 16
bush, 10

Canberra, 10
central eastern lowlands, 15, 21
cities, 9, 10
climate, 9, 10, 13, 14, 21, 23, 47
coal, 18
continents, 5–7
coral reefs, 10, 27, 31, 33

62

crocodiles (salties), 33
cuscus, spotted, *31*
cyclones, 25

Darling River, 19, 21
deserts, 23, **24**, 27–28
Devil's Marbles, 16
diamonds, 18
dingoes, 42, 43, 45, 51
Dove Lake, 18
droughts, 14, 30, 50
dugongs (sea cows), 33
dust storms, 25

earthquakes, 5, 19
eastern highlands, 15, 16
echidnas, 44, 45, **46**
emus, 9, 28
equator, 13, 14
eucalyptus trees, 29, 43–44
Europe, 5, 7
evaporative cooling, 41

feral animals, 50, 52
fires, 25, 30, 35–37
firestick farming, 30, 36, 37
foxes, 49, 50

geology, 19, 21
gibber deserts, 23
Gibson Desert, 23
gold, 18
Gondwana, 46, 47
grasslands, 27, 28, 35
grazers, 28–29
Great Artesian Basin, 21
Great Barrier Reef, 10, 31, 33
Great Dividing Range, 10, 15, *16*, 21
Great Sandy Desert, 23
Great Victorian Desert, 23

Hammersley Range, 15

Himalaya Mountains, 21
hopping mice, 28

India, 46

jellyfish, 35

kangaroos, *8*, 9, 28, 37, **38**, 40–41, **41**, 53–54
koalas, 9, 43–44
kowaris, 28

Lake Barrine, 18
Lake Eyre, 18, *19*, 27
lakes, 18, *19*, 27
land bridges, 35
latitude, 13

Macdonnell Range, 15
magma, 19
mammals, defined, 39
manatees, 33
mangrove swamps, 33
marsupials, 28, 30, **31**, 39–43, **40**
melanin, 25
minerals, 18
monitor lizards, 9
monkeys, 30
monotremes, 44–46
monsoons, 14
mountains, 5, 10, 15, *16*
Mount Kosciusko, 15
Murray River, 19, 21
Musgrave Range, 15
myxomatosis, 50–51

Nambung National Park, 16
natural disasters, 25
New Guinea, 44, 45
New South Wales, 10
New Zealand, 21, 23
nocturnal animals, 28, 43

North America, 5, 7
Northern Hemisphere, 13, 15
Northern Territory, 10
North Pole, 14

octopus, 34
Outback, 9, 10, 15, 28
ozone layer, 23–24

Panama, 7
Pangaea, 5, *6*, 46
Panthalassa, 5, *6*
para grass, 52
petroglyphs, 37
Pinnacles, 16
plants, 27–28, 30, 46, 47, 52
plate edges, 5, 19
platypus, 9–10, 44–45, *45*
pneumatocysts, 34
polar zones, 14
population, 10
possums, 30, *31*, *40*
Protesters' Falls, *20*

Queensland, 10

rabbit calcivirus disease, 51
rabbits, *48*, 49–51
rainfall, 14, 18, 21, 27, 29, 30
rain forests, 27, 30–31
red kangaroos, 40
rivers, 18–19, 21
rock formations, 15–16

sand dunes, 23, *24*, 27
savannas, 10, 27, 28
sea dragons, 34, *34*
sea grass beds, 33
seasons, 14
semidesert regions, 27–28
sharks, 35, 44
sheep, 21, 23, 50, 51, 53

Simpson Desert, 23, *24*
skin cancer, 23–25
Snowy Mountains, 15
South America, 5, 7, 46
South Australia, 10
Southern Hemisphere, 13–15
South Pole, 14
squirrel gliders, 30
starfish, 52
states and territories, 10
supercontinent, 5, *6*, 46

Tasmania, 10, 30, 44
Tasmanian devils, 43
tectonic plates, 5, 19, 21, 23, 47
temperate rain forests, 30
temperate zones, 14
termite mounds, *29*
termites, 29
toads, 53
trees, 29
tropical rain forests, 30–31
tropical zones, 14
tropic of Cancer, 14
tropic of Capricorn, 14
Twelve Apostles, 16

Uluru, 15–16, *17*
underground homes, *26*, 28

Victoria, 10
volcanoes, 5, 19, 21, 23

wallabies, 9, 28
water, 21, 23
Western Australia, 10
western plateau, 15
Wild Dog Fence, 51
wildflowers, 28, 30
wombats, 9, 28, *42*, 42–43
woodlands, 27, 29–30